The Insignificance of Being Me

Poems and Thoughts by:
Moishe Aquart

" Life is a Test ,

Life is a Trust ,

Life is a temporary assignment."

Pastor Lowell

Mother Above

Oceans -
White and Blue
Kiss the Heavens,
As they serenade the stars too.

Soil -
Shimmers of Silver and Gold.
Trees canvas the sky; brazen and bold.

The Moon conducts an Orchestra of
Wind and waves.

The Sun nurtures life each day.

Fear of Living

I have seen this world change,
So many times.
Never for the better.

Nutrition has become a religion,
And human touch a sin.
Tongue tied on morals; Our actions
Demonize emotions.

Voices are purged; only leaving
Whispers.
Zealots congregate; worshipping
Ideologies and accomplishments of vanity.

I have seen this world change,
So many times.
Never for the better.

<u>Full</u>

The Moon does not bat an eye; until
You see it smile.
Glaring, sometimes, blaring in his
modest reveal.
How we romanticize for the sake
of symbolism or compromise a
belief.

A self centered presence -
that even night, cannot bring
to its demise.
Bright.
Our eyes entranced to the
quest we see each fortnight.

Precipice

In the last days of Sunshine.
Shadows find refuge in reflections.
Stars hide in a twinkle of an eye;
as others go blind.

The twilight binds the inevitable
defeat of minds.
The sun leaves -
Darkness now has its time.

The Time Traveller

Set upon a time of decadence
and wine: I begin at the end.
Each blink is a frame of life.
Changing the continuity, that led
me here.
Holding her hand, as she held
Mine.
I dine by a single flame.
Rampant in self indulgence.

I see our Sunset; from time
to time.
Wondering how long will be
My life line.
Where does it begin; where will
it end.
I have been here before,
and I will be here again.
In Dreams and thoughts of
others.

Realizing time and space and
how it bends.

Milky Way

I found myself amongst the stars,
Wondering deep on a stream of
Thought.
Alone.
"Did I wonder too far"

The expanse I travelled of
Worlds unseen and all of
The galaxies in between.

A search for long lost
Answers; other sought.

A monolith -
In the infinite dark.

Cast away -
Flung into the Abyss
As a spark.
I hold onto the tail of a
Comet.
Adrift; amongst the Stars.

Narrow

A down trodden path -
Steps or strides, bring no end
To a wall.

Breathing in myself; I cannibalize
Air.
My reach is a standing crucifix.

I see a dim dot, that spirals
Me further.
I turn an inch, then another.

I take a path sideways,
Not facing what is in front
Of me.

__Church__

Concrete pillars -
grey to appeal.
A white Stark architecture.
Standing tall -
this tower of bruised, and
the one's charged.

A structure to stand time.
A plea; a prayer for the
have nots.

This building will stand;
concealing and Congregating
Man's investment in God.

(Pigeon Key)

My eyes had a playdate
With the beach.
Seeing swells develop the
Perfect wave; layers of blue
Carpet the surface from
Shoreline to horizon, and
The textures of the sand
And ocean.
My ears hear the wind
Sing; a lullaby to my soul.

Never Gone

Ashes blow with the wind; bringing
Home that feeling of life, that
Has come and gone.
Immortality comes with memories.
Keeping alive those images
That persist.
Ones of bliss and loving
Touches; given with a kiss.
We will reunite, when I finish.
In a sunny corner,
Of Heaven's myth.

The Long Sleep

Seeing everyday life, with my eyes closed.
My heart still has a rhythmic beat,
That others share.
All numb to God's will.

The slumber of saints, have left
The Horsemen rampant.
Mouths choke on dirt and ash;
Manifestations of bad science plague.

Waters commodity rises -
For only the wealthy to secure.
We praise disappointments, while
Chaining our independence and
Free thought.

Ones adorned in gold; stay secure
In their homes; preaching only
To make them a Matron, Martyr,
Or Messiah.

Dreams past and the future, and
The inability to understand -
Transfix our sleep.

A lullaby of non-substance and
Apathy.

We snore deep; and the feeling we
Accomplish a mission, do our job,
Or nurture unconditional.
We sleep deeper -
Ignoring cries.

The Ambition of Fire

Smoldering moods -
Evoke the sense of mortality.

Embers crackle red -
Communing a flame.

Warmth comforts fierce intentions.

Smoke instigates confrontation;
Less a breathe.
Only charred emotions.

<u>Steam</u>

Dreams of other worlds;
Sabotage the subconscious, as
Reality drains the day.

The Solace of night, doesn't
Expound pain and regret.

Each night; Each World
Is a tempest.
Erasing the conscious sense of purpose.

Worlds of dark water and
Sensual pleasures; erode the
Idea to wake.

Each night dreams release
The Steam.

<u>Dragon</u>

Scales fall from fire.
As the day illuminates Rose Red.
Chariots pull the need; while knights
Fall beside.

Behold this beauty.
Angelic of Crimson and Cinder.
Breathing the soot -
So desired.

Love Laid Under the Sun

I will find you in that place,
Where lilies and Doves meet.
On that road; within each mile -
I hear a heartbeat.
Closer to her lips, my thoughts dangle,
Until we kiss.

Molded of Mud; I give a rib
To a myth.
Love lies under the Sun.
Fires born, until your return.

A figure imaginary -
My love you invite my soul.
To a union; that cannot be undone.

Plain View

I built a Church far away, so
The UnGodly could not find their way.

Built on a plain; where only
Straw and mud laid.
Bells ring out, to Sound the Day;
For all who have strayed.

Food and Drink; I give to take.
Equal hospitality for those who stay.

On this ground I made.
Saints and Sinners, have no say.

This Church is built for the
Meek and mild; for them to lay.

The Boy
and the Bee's Nest

Don't touch -
She said.
The curious boy; gleeful from
Cheek to cheek.
Kept poking and prodding.
A violation of their space.

The boy snickered; and sped
Up his pace.
He was a monstrosity; to
Their placid state.

Simple little lives; congregating
Under a crown.

Provoked; they repel with only
Deadly fire.

One more swing, the boy thought. A grievous mistake;
As he span in terrible wrought.

Don't touch -
She said.
.

The Eye of Andromeda

I saw a star,
So bright; so far.
In all the blackness -
It shone on me.
Singled out -
My heart found a new route.
North of other constellations,
That charted the sky.

A princess crowned with a
Galactic halo.
Her luminosity pulled me -
Spiralling to collide.

Gravitating to her design,
I wished upon this star.
Traveling by her side.
However far.

The Life of Peter Pan

"How," have I seen myself grow old.
When I remember being so young,
Age has crept up on me,
Like a game of hide and seek.
I'm it -
But not for long.

The love that comforted as
A youth; dissipates in the
Breath of my mother and father
The memories they leave me
Are ghosts of my senses.

I remember myself; as that
Boy, at that age.
Nothing was corrupt.

Now I celebrate every day;
Above the dirt.
Living in the instant.

Into the Wilderness

Hearts expound on a plain of
Self doubt; as tragedy surround
Thought. Unfound.
Look for me in the dark; along
With mushrooms and sprouts.
I go further into the wilderness;
Shrugging off twigs and limbs.
I watch fawns and pixies that
Are all around.
Complicit without a sound.
I go further into the wilderness.
Not lost; just not found.

The Poet and Thief

Stolen heart scribed by others.
Ones who loved and lost.
Scriptures dedicated to Oohs and Aahs.
A time when dying was heroic and glorious.
Tales told to make mine.
Lauding with a devilish smile.

Land of Wolves

In the Land of Wolves; the
Weak are meat, so the strong
Can eat.
Smothering humanity -
Strangling civility -
Undoing principals God taught.

Packs gather under a dark agenda.
Clandestine, they should be feared;
Not sought.
Hunger is the motive that
Dictates their heart.

So Savage -
Claws and fangs; scrape the bones.
Howls cry out; setting the moon
As a symbol of clout.

Parasite

I looked in the Mirror to see
Myself; what I saw was someone
Else.
I looked deeper; to see if it
Was me; but it was something
That wanted to be me.

I closed my eyes, and then opened
Them to see; but all I felt was
Cold hands holding me.
Its hands covered my eyes;
So there would be no more
Of me.

I cannot see myself anymore;
Or the man I wanted to
Be.

The Opus of Ascension

I am leaving this place -
Where I have been too long.
Treading above, the daily dilemma
Of the Soul.
Regrets reside here.
Empathy chains me; to prolonging the
Inevitable, as complacency leaves
Me unsettled.

Stepping upward, out of this hole
Hands reach out; for trust.
For the love of me and
Others; a bond amongst one
Another.
Held up: to elevate to a higher place.
To see life, as I embrace it
With Faith.

I hear a melody; the makes
Me rediscover -
Up is the only way to go.